Eve

By L. Nembhard

Copyright 2024 Lateefah Nembhard

This book is a work of fiction. Any references to historical events, real people, or real places are used fictitiously. Other names, characters, places, and events are products of the author's imagination and any resemblance to actual events or places or persons, living or dead is entirely coincidental.

Chapter 1

Eight-year-old Lilly stood in her uncle's garden where it was hot and humid. The sun was bright, and Lilly swayed back and forth happily in the hot sun eating an ice cream. Her golden hair glinted in the sunlight and fell on the shoulders of her yellow summer dress. Her dress swung slowly brushing against her knees as she took the last few bites of her ice-cream cone. She began skipping through the grass. The garden was quite large with one big tree near the back of the garden. There was a large cement patio on the ground surrounded by grass that stretched far back into the garden.

The blades of grass brushed Lilly's bare toes poking out from her white pair of flower-patterned open-toe sandals. She skipped faster and started running until she reached the tall tree which was being used to tie a long washing line in place. As she did, the tip of her sandal got caught on a small rock in the garden causing her to fall over into the dirt. As Lilly sat upright in the dirt, the small particles of dirt fell from her fingers, she brushed her hands together and checked her knees. There was no damage, just more dirt to brush off. With her legs outstretched in front of her, she began brushing herself off while still sat in the dirt. Lilly hummed a little tune to herself thinking about how proud her mother would be that she didn't make a fuss about falling over this time. She pressed her hands behind her with her arms bone straight to get up. Her small fingers spread wide across the dirt as she stood herself up. Lilly heard a voice. "I love you," it said.

Lilly whipped her head around and got up quickly to look around. Her yellow dress was dirty now and she thought about what her mother might say. "Hello?" she said in response to the voice with her eyebrows raised.

There was no reply, just the sound of the birds above in the trees surrounding the garden. She looked up and squinted her eyes as the sun beamed down on her. She was next to a large oak tree; she took a step forward so she could peek around the tree to see if she could figure out where the voice came from. As her feet pushed against the dirt, she heard it again "I love you". She looked down at her small feet in confusion taking a closer look. Her feet were also quite dirty now and she wiggled her toes to try and remove the excess dirt. She then jumped on the spot and heard the voice again. She noticed something was making noise in the dirt directly underneath her feet and she began to investigate. She looked ahead of her and saw a small stick that had fallen away from the tree. She picked it up and returned to the suspicious area where the noise had come from, and she began poking at the ground with the stick. Something firm but soft was underneath the dirt. She moved the stick around and scraped the ground trying to clear as much dirt as possible. With some of the dirt now cleared she could see a piece of what looked like a clear blue plastic bag poking out from the ground. She dropped the stick and used her hands to pull at the plastic.

The more she pulled, the more the dirt came away and she could make out what appeared to be the face of a doll. Lilly planted her feet wide on the ground and used all her strength to pull at the bag. When the bag was finally released from the ground, she took her hands and brushed the blue plastic revealing the doll's full face and clothes. From what she could make out behind the plastic cover, the doll was quite tall and had a baby pink dress on with white lace sewn along the hem of the dress. It also had red and white stripey tights. The doll was life-sized and had long brown hair and deep dark brown eyes, she stared at the eyes for a moment, and they stared back at her. She noticed that the eyes on this doll were nothing like the ones she had seen on her toy doll at home. The one at home had thick black eyelashes, a bit like a bristle brush but thinner, and it had blue eyes that sometimes rolled open and closed easily if you were to move the doll a little. The eyes on this doll, looked a little droopy and almost sad. She hugged the doll and the voice sounded again "I love you". She looked at the doll once more holding her arms out straight and then proceeded to rip open the plastic covering the doll. The plastic was quite thick, but she managed to make a tiny opening and continued pulling on the edges of the rip she had made. Eventually, the plastic gave way a little, and she managed to get one of the doll's arms out of the plastic. One long arm covered in a long pink sleeve, flopped out of the plastic bag. Realising it was going to be a struggle to open the bag, Lilly picked up the bag and ran towards her uncle's house with the hot sun still beating against her face and back. Reaching a spot where the door was, she found shade and sat on the step for a moment to take a rest. She turned the doll in the bag looking at the back and the front, one arm of it still flopping outside of the bag. Lilly then stood up and reached for the door handle that led into the house. The handle felt slightly warm from the heat, she pressed down and opened the door with the doll tucked under her other arm. Once she was through the back door, she stood in the hallway deciding if it was best to try the kitchen first or the living room to seek out an adult who could help her with her new discovery. The hallway had cream-coloured wallpaper and laminated light brown wooden flooring.

 There was an old cabinet against the wall stacked with old ornaments and random boxes and papers. The tiny pieces of dry dirt from Lilly's sandals peppered the floor as she walked towards the kitchen. In the kitchen, Lilly found her mom whose name was Kathy, leaning over a soapy washing-up bowl with her rubber yellow gloves on. Her mother who was in her forties had brown hair and kind brown eyes, she wore a blue silk blouse and white trousers. Kathy had long brown hair that reached her elbows. Lilly's uncle's wife whose name was Dianne, was also in the kitchen. Dianne was at the kitchen counter peeling potatoes with her back to the room. Dianne had short black hair which was styled into a pixie cut. She wore a beige T-shirt and dark blue denim shorts. She too was in her forties like Kathy Lilly's mom. Lilly's uncle whose name was Shaun, had inherited the house from Lilly's great-grandmother. Lilly's uncle Shaun lived in the house with his wife Dianne, and they had no children of their own. Lilly and her mother Kathy who was

Uncle Shaun's sister had come over to the house to spend the day there.

Lilly loved spending time with family, it was a regular thing they did where the adults would always cook together, and Lilly would always play in the large garden. Lilly's uncle Shaun was standing near the stove cooking food. He was in a dark green t-shirt with light blue denim jeans, he had light brown hair and similar eyes to Lilly's mum Kathy. Shaun was tall and had broad shoulders, he stood over the kitchen stove with his sleeves rolled up. "Mom, I found something in the garden!" Lilly said loudly. Her mom looked over to her, "What did you find Lilly?" Lilly responded excitedly "I found a toy doll; can I keep it? Can you open it for me?" Shaun, Lilly's uncle turned around briefly from the stove and glimpsed to see what it was. "You found a doll?" Shaun asked with curiosity. "Yes, and it has a pink dress on", Lilly said trying to hand the doll over to her mom. "Let me see", Kathy said pulling off her rubber gloves and surveying the dirty plastic. Kathy pulled at the plastic and took out the doll, its pink dress and long brown hair was pristine, seemingly preserved by the thick blue plastic it had been wrapped in. "Where did you find it?" asked Kathy Lilly's mom. Lilly responded eagerly, "At the back of the garden, I fell down, and then I heard a noise and then I was digging, and I found it". Kathy looked confused "You heard a noise?" asked Kathy. "Yes" Lilly nodded enthusiastically, "she said I Love you". Lilly quickly placed her small hands on the doll's stomach and pressed down to show her mom how it worked. "See...she talks". Kathy scanned the doll's face and then replied, "She looks so…realistic". "So can I keep her, is she mine?" Lilly asked eagerly. Kathy thought for a moment and then replied, "Well maybe, unless your uncle wants her. It's his garden". She smiled and looked over at Lilly's uncle Shaun. Shaun shrugged his shoulders and continued tending to the food on the stove. "I don't mind, you can keep it, but maybe stick it in the washing machine first, who knows how long that thing's been outside."

"Yes, let's wash her, then you can keep her". Kathy put the doll in the washing machine and filled the tray with washing powder. Lilly trailed behind her mom, observing closely as the washing machine door shut, and the circular window began to fill with sudsy water. As the doll circled within the machine, its face pressed against the glass, revealing its eyes peering out through the round window. Lilly remained captivated, fixated on the doll's mesmerizing rotation. "I'm going to name her Eve", she said.

Chapter 2

Night-time came and Lilly fell asleep in the car on the way home. Lilly's dad Ben had picked them up from their uncle's home. Ben had a slim build with blue eyes and dark chestnut brown hair, he had a thick beard and wore navy blue-rimmed glasses. Once they pulled up to their home, Ben put Lilly to bed. He carefully carried Lilly up the stairs and tucked the doll she'd named Eve next to her under the pink butterfly-patterned duvet. Lilly's room was cosy and with pink painted walls, white butterflies were stencilled on the wall and there were stick-on moons and stars that were scattered across the ceiling of the bedroom. She had a fluffy pink rug in the middle of the floor and a toy box full of many toys and doll accessories alongside a pine chest of drawers that Ben had carefully painted white.
Ben switched on Lilly's lamp turned off her main light and closed her bedroom door.

Ben and Kathy sat together downstairs on the leather cream sofa together watching tv as Lilly slept upstairs. Kathy and Ben chatted about their day while curled up on the sofa. Ben heard a shuffling noise, and he looked up at the ceiling, "I think she's out of bed" he said to Kathy. Kathy sighed and said, "I'll go". She then got up and started making her way into the corridor. The stairway was situated right next to the small kitchen in the house and the moonlight from the kitchen window shone on the bottom steps. When Kathy arrived at the foot of the stairs, she looked up at the top of the stairs, in the darkness Kathy could make out a small shadow of a figure, stood at the top of the stairs, "Lilly, go to bed darling", Kathy said as she found the passage light with her finger and pressed it. It didn't switch on. Kathy flicked it a few more times to no avail and spoke again, "Lilly...have you had a bad dream?" There was no answer and then Kathy heard small footsteps running away. Kathy climbed the stairs determined to reach the other light switch for the upstairs passageway. As Kathy reached the top of the stairs, she flicked the light switch on and headed for Lilly's bedroom door. The light flooded the empty passageway that led to the bedrooms. The door creaked as she slowly opened the door to peek in. Lilly was in her bed and had her arm wrapped around her newfound doll. Kathy pulled the covers over Lilly and whispered her name to see if she was awake. "Lilly?" Lilly was sound asleep and didn't respond. Kathy looked confused and watched for a moment as Lilly slept peacefully, her blanket rose and fell as she breathed in her deep sleep.

Kathy quietly closed the door and left the room. She switched off the passage light and descended the stairs. As Kathy reached the final step at the bottom of the stairs, she heard the familiar creak of Lilly's bedroom door upstairs. Kathy sighed and said "Lilly, are you awake?" she then turned towards the staircase and stared into the darkness waiting for a response. There was only silence for a moment and then Kathy heard, "I love you". This wasn't Lilly's voice, it sounded exactly like Lilly's doll. But Kathy was confused as to why it sounded so loud since the doll was with Lilly in her bedroom. Kathy squinted her eyes to try and focus, and as she peered into the darkness, she could just make out a pair of legs covered in red and white stripey tights, standing at the top of the stairs. Kathy took one slow step up onto the stairs and it creaked as she did. "Hello!" Kathy said sharply. Kathy waited for an answer but all she could hear was a light raspy breath as if someone was struggling to breathe. Kathy was getting worried now, her heart began beating quickly and she froze not knowing whether she should take another step. Then she felt a hand on her shoulder and let out a gasp as she pulled in her breath, "You alright?" Ben said. Kathy turned towards Ben, "Don't do that, you scared me". Ben looked confused and said, "You've been ages, has Lilly gone to bed now?" Kathy didn't answer and looked back at the top of the stairs with a blank look on her face. Ben switched on the passage light beside her and as the stairs lit up, she could see that there was nothing there.

"Kathy…?" Ben said now looking concerned. "Yes, she's in her bed, and she looked like she was knocked out asleep. It's just…I heard her bedroom door open upstairs, so I thought she came back out of her bed and this light wasn't working before, so I had to…" Ben interrupted "Kathy…" he whispered.

Kathy lapsed into silence; her attention drawn to the direction Ben was facing. His gaze was fixed on the kitchen window overlooking the garden. A rhythmic screech emanated from outside, suggesting a back-and-forth movement. "Who on earth is that on the swing out there?" Ben exclaimed.

Looking outside they could see what appeared to be a small child facing away from the house swinging on their garden swing. The house was so silent they could hear pin drop, they could hear the familiar squeaky sound of the swing moving. The legs that were moving back and forth on the swing were covered in red and white stripey tights. Quickening their pace, they rushed to the kitchen door that led to the garden and Ben promptly turned the key in the lock. "Something strange is going on," said Kathy as she peered outside of the dark kitchen window, she had a look of fear on her face, and her gaze was fixed on the garden swing. As Ben finally released the kitchen door leading to the garden, he scanned his eyes around in the darkness outside. The garden was still and there was no one sat on the swing, it was a hot stuffy summers night so there was no wind blowing.

He turned to Kathy with a crazy look in his eyes, "Kathy, please tell me you saw what I saw?" Said Ben. Kathy nodded silently and then spoke, "Yes, I did, there was a child out there…a girl". Ben looked pale, "I'm going to check on Lilly" he said and before Kathy could respond to tell him about the figure that she saw on the stairs he was already halfway up. After a few minutes, Ben returned downstairs, "She's in bed, she's fine" he said. He took another look out of the kitchen window and made sure the door was locked again. "Let's just get an early night and go to bed" he said to Kathy. Kathy agreed and they made their way to their room.

In the dark under the duvet, Kathy tossed and turned in her bed, she couldn't sleep. She kept dreaming of a girl in the garden. Ben tried to hold her, "Get some sleep" he whispered in a sleepy voice. The more Kathy tried to fall asleep the more it seemed impossible. After what seemed like hours, she opened her eyes and stared at the clock on the night stand it was 3am. Disappointed that it was way too early to get up she squeezed her eyes shut trying to force herself to fall back to sleep.

The room was silent and dark, only the moonlight lit up a corner of the bedroom. Once again, Kathy could hear the swing in the garden moving back and forth. Kathy's eyes peeled open slowly as she listened, "Don't look… just go to sleep" she thought to herself. She closed her eyes again and felt Ben's hand stroking her hair. Eyes still closed she attempted to snuggle up to him but then stopped when she realised, he was sleeping with his back towards her. If his back was facing her, then who was stroking her hair? She opened her eyes in a panic, the sound of the bedroom door creaked, and she turned on the lamp beside the bed. The room was empty, but the door was ajar, and she was sure she had closed it. Kathy quickly shook Ben to wake him up. "Ben, please wake up!" she said still panicking. Ben awoke slowly, "What's up?" he whispered.

"Something, or someone was in our room" Kathy said in a shaky voice, "Someone was stroking my hair". She had tears in her eyes now as she realised how crazy she sounded. Ben held her tightly and she burst into tears. "I don't know what's going on but something's not right…ever since we took that doll home…". Ben pulled her away from his chest for a moment and looked Kathy in the eyes confused. "The doll?" he said. Kathy nodded slowly "Yes, the doll…I wanted to tell you before, but I didn't want to freak you out even more, I saw it at the top of the stairs standing on its own…I wasn't sure what I was seeing but when you turned the light on it wasn't there anymore. I thought it was just my mind playing tricks on me but then you said you saw the girl in the garden and that girl or whatever it was had stripey red tights on just like the doll". She whimpered as she spoke. "I know it sounds crazy…" Ben cut her off "No…you're not crazy we both saw a girl on our swing outside and then she just disappeared. Let's throw that doll away and take Lilly shopping in the morning for a new one, that way she won't be so upset about not having the doll anymore." Ben whispered. "I think that's a really good idea," said Kathy nodding through her tears. "Right, I'll do it now" said Ben climbing out of bed. He wasted no time; swiftly, he located the doll near Lilly's bedside, descended straight downstairs, and promptly discarded it in the outdoor bin. The doll's mournful eyes seemed to gaze up at him as he closed the lid. When Ben finally got back into bed, both him and Kathy didn't get much sleep, but Ben held onto Kathy as tightly as he could until the morning came.

When Kathy and Ben woke up in the morning, the first thing they did was check on Lilly again. Lilly stretched out her arms with a big smile on her face. It was Sunday and she looked outside her bedroom window and saw how warm it was outside. Ben was downstairs sorting breakfast and Kathy was laying out clothes for Lilly to wear in her bedroom. "Morning sweetie", Kathy said to Lilly "How did you sleep?". Lilly didn't answer, she was too busy looking under her bed and lifting her duvet as though she had lost something.

Lilly finally spoke, "Mummy, Where's Eve? I can't find her she's gone". Kathy abruptly stopped fussing with the clothes and then turned to Lilly. "Darling, I wanted to talk to you about Eve, me and daddy think maybe you would like a new doll from the shops instead because Eve is a bit old". Lilly pushed out her lower lip and frowned before responding. "But I don't want a new doll, I want Eve; Eve isn't that old".

Lilly spoke while pushing her feet through the leggings her mum had laid out on the bed for her.

Kathy took a deep breath and sighed. She stroked Lilly's arm. "How about we go to the shops, and you can pick any doll you like?", Kathy looked at Lilly's face hoping for a positive response. "I don't know", said Lilly as she pulled a pink summer dress over her face. "Where is Eve anyway?", Lilly asked again. Kathy looked towards the floor feeling guilty as she knew she had to lie to her daughter's face and said, "Me and daddy put her away for safe keeping, let's get breakfast now". Kathy said quickly changing the subject. They began making their way downstairs to meet Ben at the kitchen table. Kathy stepped slowly down the stairs and felt a sense of calm. Lilly had gone ahead and had already taken her seat. Kathy reached the doorway of the kitchen and gasped. Lilly shouted excitedly, "I found her mummy!". Lilly was adjusting the doll as it was seated in the chair at the small 4-seater breakfast table. Kathy locked eyes with Ben as he turned around to face her. She quickly walked over to Ben and whispered, "Did you take the doll out of the bin?" Ben shook his head slowly and whispered back, "No".

Kathy looked at the doll and it seemed to stare back at her, with its big eyes and solemn expression. She whispered to Ben again so that Lilly wouldn't hear. "Ben, we need to do something about this, I'm not going to be able to sleep with that thing here. It's too creepy and no one will believe us if we tell them what's been happening". Ben agreed and they both decided the best thing to do would be to drive back to Lilly's uncles house and bury the doll again in the garden where Lilly had found it.

Chapter 3

Lilly fell asleep while they drove in the car. The Doll was strapped into the seat next to Lilly who had insisted on it. Kathy kept looking in the mirror expecting to catch to doll the moving, but she never did. "We can talk now, she's asleep" said Ben looking at Lilly in the rear-view mirror. Kathy responded, "I want to ask my brother about this in case he knows anything, maybe his experienced something weird at the house but just never told us". Ben nodded, "True, but I'm sure he would have said something about the doll before you took it home, If Shaun knew something wasn't right surely, he wouldn't just let you take it".

They soon pulled up at Shaun's house and Kathy knocked on the door. Shaun quickly answered the door and invited them in. Ben picked up Lilly who was now awake but a little sleepy, she held on tightly to her doll as her dad carried her from the car indoors. Ben left Lilly in the living room watching cartoons with her doll while the adults all gathered in the kitchen. Kathy and Ben explained all the strange things that had happened, and Shaun looked at Kathy and Ben like they were deluded. "I'm sorry, but I just can't believe that all of this is because of that toy doll, are you sure you weren't just tired and imagining things?". Dianne, Shaun's wife who had been listening intently at the kitchen table without uttering a word finally spoke up and said, "They are not imagining things Shaun". Her fingers started shaking as she looked at all of them with desperation. She then faced Shaun with a stern expression and took a deep breath. "Remember when I used to tell you I could hear a noise in the garden, every time I went to collect the washing from the line near the tree at the back, I could hear laughter…like a child or someone playing." Kathy, Shaun, and Ben were all transfixed on Dianne. She continued, "At the time it seemed so innocent. I mean it's a garden, I just thought it was a neighbour's kids or something until one day…" She looked at them all in the eyes one by one and then looked back down at her hands. Dianne continued. "One day, before I even got outside, I could hear the laughter really loud and clear and when I looked outside, I saw a girl at the back of the garden running around the tree, she then stopped and peered out from behind the big oak tree as though she was playing a game of hide and seek. She wasn't dressed like the kids from nowadays she had a pink dress on…"

"…and Red stripey tights". Kathy interrupted finishing the sentence for her and turned to Ben for acknowledgement. Ben's face held an expression of disbelief. Dianne nodded. "I called out to the girl but then as I walked outside, she disappeared…right in front of my eyes." The room fell silent. Shaun placed a hand over his wife Dianne's trembling hands. Ben broke the silence first, "Have you seen or heard anything since?" Dianne looked up and said, "No, after that, it went away…there was no laughter nothing, I stopped taking the clothes outside anyway because I was so freaked out and I started using the dryer more instead". Shaun looked at his sister Kathy and said, "I never saw it myself…or heard the laughter she was talking about, but I do remember Dianne mentioning seeing a girl in the garden and I just didn't take it too seriously. She said it had stopped and so we just moved on and forgot about it". Shaun looked at Kathy with a guilty expression on his face. "I should have taken her more seriously. Can I see the doll?" Shaun asked.

Kathy nodded and went into the living room to get the doll. "I just need to borrow Eve for a minute darling", she said to Lilly. Lilly replied, "Will you bring her back soon? We're watching TV together". Kathy nodded in response and made her way back into the kitchen. She handed the doll to her brother Shaun. Shaun studied the doll turning it over and then back again, his gaze left the doll and he started to look up as if he was trying to remember something. "What is it?", said Kathy "I don't know", said Shaun, "something about it looks familiar but I just can't remember why". Without saying another word, he gasped slightly and held up his finger as if he'd remembered something but needed a minute. Shaun then walked over to the old cabinet in the corridor that led to the kitchen. He opened the cabinet draws and grabbed something before walking back over to everyone at the kitchen table. He dropped the doll on the table and Kathy, Ben, and Dianne's eyes followed his every move looking puzzled. Shaun placed an old metal box on the table. It looked like it was originally decorated with green flowers, but all the patterns that were once there had eroded overtime. Shaun opened the metal box and scattered the contents onto the table. A stack of photos fell onto the table. Ben, Kathy's husband quickly picked up a photo that lay on the table and then looked at Kathy. "Is this you Kathy?", He pointed to a girl who looked exactly like Kathy. Kathy peered closer at the photo and before she could answer, Shaun answered for her. "It's not Kathy, it's our grandmother…Ethel", Shaun said. Ben looked astonished "Wow, Kathy she looks exactly like you, the hair and everything". In the photo, Kathy and Shaun's grandmother was stood outside by a tree, the same tree that they could still see now in the garden. In the photo, Ethel appeared to be somewhere in her thirties and had shoulder-length brown hair. "Our grandmother Ethel grew up in this house". Shaun said and started laying the photos out neatly on the table, turning them over so everyone could see them.

"There it is", Shaun said pointing to another photo. "That doll, in almost every photo Grandma Ethel is holding that doll, I knew I'd seen it somewhere, but I just couldn't remember where". The photos all looked quite similar in that Grandma Ethel would be either in the garden holding the doll or inside the house, sat on the sofa with the doll on her lap. Ethel could be seen in the photo cradling the doll, as though she was looking after it. Kathy was shocked and began scanning her eyes across each photo. "Why so many photos with the doll?" Kathy questioned, with her eyes meeting Shaun's with a look of concern. Shaun didn't have an answer and looked back at Kathy with the same confused expression. Dianne eventually broke the silence, when she held one photo up with her hands shaking and said, "This one isn't a doll". Everyone turned to look at the photo Dianne held up. "It's a little girl," said Shaun. Kathy looked closer at the photo, "Oh my god she's wearing the same outfit", Kathy said almost in a whisper. She looked at Shaun who exchanged the same look of confusion with her. "Do you have any idea who this girl is?" asked Kathy. Shaun shook his head and said "No, but we can ask Mum". Kathy chimed in again "Maybe it's mum in the photo, it looks like it could be her, maybe she just had the outfit and the doll and Grandma Ethel put the clothes on the doll when she grew out of them". Kathy looked around the table at everyone to see if they agreed. They were all sat down now in their seats, Shaun nodded and then pulled out his mobile phone.

He then dialled his and Kathy's mother's number and then put the phone on loudspeaker. They all listened intently waiting for an answer, it was still light outside, it had only just reached 1 pm so they weren't expecting her to be asleep. The phone rang for what seemed like an eternity before Shaun and Kathy's mother picked up. They could hear fumbling and then the Facetime picture came on, but it was dark. "Hello, is that you Shaun?" said Lilly's grandma. Shaun breathed a sigh of relief. "Yes, mum it's me, well actually Kathy's here too, we just wanted to ask you about something quickly, I hope you're well…could you hold out the phone in front of you then you can see my face on Facetime". Lilly's Grandma replied, "Yes, I'm fine, sorry I had the phone to my ear, I'm not used to this technology. I've been out in the garden most of the morning just enjoying the heat, your dad's cooking on the barbecue just now. There's too much smoke so I've come indoors for now. What is it, is everything ok you sound unsettled?" Shaun's gaze met Kathy's; their mother could almost always tell when something was wrong. Shaun responded, "Well, we found some old photos of Grandma Ethel…and there's a little girl in one of them. We were hoping you could tell us who the little girl is, we thought maybe it was you…as a child". As Shaun spoke, he held up the photo with the child in the pink dress and stripey tights. Lilly's Grandma squinted at the screen until the photo came into focus. "Where did you find that photo?" Lilly's Grandma asked in a stern voice. Kathy answered this time, "It was in a box mum, with a bunch of other photos, we just wanted to check if the girl in this picture is you?" Lilly's Grandma was silent for a moment and then said, "It's not me in the photo it's …it's your aunt my older sister, you've never met her…please put the photo back where you found it". Lilly's Grandma sounded hostile. Kathy replied, "But mum you don't have an older sister."

"She's dead Kathy, she died when she was around ten years old, she fell down the well in the garden, I don't keep any photos of her. Please put it back." Lilly's Grandma said looking upset now. "I'm so sorry Mum, we didn't know", Shaun said. "Where did you find those photos?" Lilly's Grandma asked curiously. Shaun answered, "They were in a green rusty tin, on that cabinet near the stairs, we found lots of photos with Grandma holding a doll". Shaun scanned the mobile phone camera over the table so Lilly's Grandma could see some of the photos. Lilly's Grandma became silent. "Don't do anything, I'm coming over", she said and abruptly ended the call. Shaun and Kathy looked at each other baffled. "Mum knows something, I've never seen her so lost for words," Kathy said, "I agree," said Shaun.

Lilly's Grandma arrived quickly within twenty minutes at the house. Shaun opened the door to his mother, Lilly's grandma whose name was Heather. Lilly's Grandma Heather had brown hair but with grey streaks in between the strands. She wore a pair of cream linen trousers and a shirt. She stepped inside and went straight to the kitchen, and without greeting anyone, she looked at Shaun directly and said, "Give me the photos", she held out her hand with a serious expression on her face. Kathy broke the awkward silence. "Mum, can you please tell us a bit more, why are there so many photos with this doll", Kathy said. Lilly's Grandma looked around and then said, "Has anything happened? Anything strange that you can't quite explain?" Kathy, Dianne, Shaun, and Ben nodded in unison. Kathy started to speak, "Lilly found this old doll wrapped in plastic in the garden and ever since…things have been weird at home, and we just want to know what's going on". Lilly's Grandma realised the doll was on the table. "Burn it!" Said Lilly's Grandma, "You need to burn it now!" They wasted no time and took the doll outside along with the photos. Shaun started up a fire in the metal bin they normally used to burn cardboard outside, and Ben helped him. Lilly's grandma threw the doll into the fire without hesitation, and Lilly who had silently followed everyone outside, stood watching by the door to see what was going on, "No, my doll!" she cried. "Why are you burning her?" Kathy rushed over to Lilly making an attempt to bring Lilly back inside the house, but it was too late, she had already seen. Kathy kept trying to hold Lilly, but Lilly pushed her away and sat on the steps outside in the garden, with her face in her hands sobbing. Kathy thought it best to leave her alone she would never be able to fully explain. Lilly's Grandma continued to act with no hesitation, and she threw the photos in without even looking at them and watched them slowly burn. She looked up at Shaun and spoke slowly.

"I thought these photos no longer existed, but it turns out they did. Your grandma Ethel was obsessed with this doll after my sister died. Your grandfather, couldn't pry that doll from your grandmother's fingers, she was so attached." Her voice broke and tears filled Lilly's grandma's eyes as she continued. "It was a terrible accident, I got the doll for my birthday when I was a little girl, but I hardly ever played with it, and my sister she wanted the doll for herself. It sounds bad but I think when I came along, she was jealous that I sometimes had more toys than her. She would take the doll from my room all the time and play with it and we would fight over it. She would carry it around with her everywhere like she owned it, and when I would catch her with it, I'd snatch it back off her. There used to be a well in the garden, right underneath this patio. We played outside in the garden a lot so, for safety, your grandfather covered the hole over with a few planks of wood. One winter, the wood must of…must have become wet and rotten, because a gap had formed where some of the wood had fell through. One day, when it was quite icy outside me, and my sister were in the garden playing and my sister was dangling the doll over the well. She was teasing me and threatening to drop it down the gap. I remember she had this horrid grin on her face, she didn't look right. I was irritated but I didn't mean for anyone to get hurt.

I tried to snatch the doll from her, and she jerked backwards to avoid me and then slipped on the icy floor and fell backwards onto the rotten wood. It snapped so easily, and she fell down the well, she still had a firm grasp on the doll, and it fell with her. I heard a splash as she hit the bottom and screamed…the way she screamed I will never forget it. I was frozen in shock, I tried to speak and shout for our parents, but nothing was coming out of my mouth. I could hear my sister gasping for her breath deep down in the well…it echoed. I could hear the doll's voice as it tumbled down the well and hit the brick saying I love you. By the time my parents heard the commotion and realised what had happened, nobody could save her….one minute my sister was teasing me and then she was gone." Lilly's grandma looked at everyone with tears rolling down her cheeks. She continued. "They retrieved her remains from the well along with the doll. Everyone was distraught... especially my mother. From that moment your grandmother was so full of grief. She needed an outlet, something to make her feel close to my sister again, so she latched onto the doll, she even put my sister's clothes on the doll, and she took it everywhere with her…" her voice trailed off as the flames on the bonfire grew and everyone stood listening silently. Lilly's Grandma continued, "I tried to tell your grandmother Ethel that since my sister had died, a little girl kept appearing in my bedroom at night. She would stand in the corner, breathing heavily and gasping for breath as though she was drowning. I couldn't see her face at first, but I could recognise those red stripey tights anywhere. They always stood out, even in the dark. I told my mother it looked just like my sister, it even dressed like her in those clothes, but it wasn't her". Lilly's Grandma shook her head.

"It was something else…something evil. Your grandmother wouldn't listen to me, she never said it out loud, but I think she blamed me for the accident. Your grandfather was roped into taking photos all the time…constantly. Your grandmother really believed my sister was somehow living inside that doll or that somehow, she could be closer to her spirit. After she put my sister's clothes on it…she would hold it constantly and she would tell me I had to play with my sister and be nice to her. We all knew the doll wasn't right, it was like it was attached to a bad spirit. But my mother wouldn't listen. She kept the doll with her everywhere she went. Night-time was terrible, I could never sleep. I would wake up in a cold sweat every night and eventually…instead of seeing that little girl standing in the corner…she would be next to me in my bed just staring at me sleeping, that's when I saw her face properly. She had a grin so wide, and her eyes were sad and droopy…" Lilly's Grandma looked straight at Kathy. "You, look like your grandmother so much Kathy, you could pass as her twin. Things at home got so bad that one day, your grandfather just said enough was enough. While your grandmother was sleeping, he took the doll, and he buried it in the garden by that tree over there". Lilly's Grandma pointed towards the large tree in the garden "…and when he did, whatever was haunting me finally stopped…and your grandmother almost just snapped out of it…at first, she kept asking about the doll but then she moved on, and we never spoke about it again.

I never saw the thing that looked like my sister again. I had put it all to the back of my mind…until you showed me those photos. My sister died in that outfit, so my mother felt like she had to keep the last thing she had worn. It didn't take me long to figure out who it was when I saw the pink dress and stripey tights…It all came flooding back to me like a bad dream. I eventually grew up, moved out and I never mentioned her to anyone because…because it was just too painful, and I never thought anyone would believe me anyway". Lilly's Grandma sobbed now, she couldn't talk anymore, and Shaun placed an arm around his mother's shoulder to comfort her.

In a solemn ceremony, they burned the doll until it was just ashes, watching as the flames consumed the red and white stripey tights and the haunted gaze of its eyes. As the last embers flickered, a chilling hush fell over everyone in the garden. Just then, a soft, haunting voice echoed through the air. "I love you," the voice whispered, but this time it emanated from Lilly herself, who stood in the corner with an eerie smile so wide, she resembled a cartoon character. The once-familiar features of Lilly's face now held a distant, otherworldly gaze.

Everyone was frozen with fear, as they realized that destroying the doll had unleashed something far more sinister. Lilly, or what appeared to be Lilly, stepped forward and placed her arms around Kathy's waist, uttering words that sent shivers down Kathy's spine. "I found my way back Mommy, just like you promised." With a horrified look on her face, Lilly's grandma turned to face Lilly and said, "Eve?"

Printed in Dunstable, United Kingdom